Ladies' Choice

Ladies' Choice

A Collection of Humor by Maine Women

edited by
Mavis Patterson

Illustrated by Melinda Wing-Horton

Thorndike Press • Thorndike, Maine

Library of Congress Cataloging in Publication Data:

Main entry under title:

Ladies' choice.

1. American wit and humor—Maine. 2. American wit and humor—Women authors. I. Patterson, Mavis, 1948- .

PN6162.L23 814'.54'0809287 82-5533
ISBN 0-89621-066-9 AACR2

Acknowledgements

"How'd Ye Know I Came from Maine" was first published in *Upcountry,* a publication of the Eagle Press, Pittsfield, Massachusetts.

Cover design by Melinda Horton.

To Fanny Fern
and broad grins

Preface

Why an anthology of humor by Maine women, you ask? Simple... well, not too simple... actually not so simple at all. The idea of a collection emerged from a discussion with members of a planning committee that was working to establish a resource center for women. It was mentioned that one of Twentieth Century woman's needs was to learn to laugh, lightheartedly, and to express her sense of humor. That suggestion launched two years of research on the concept of women and humor in general and evolved into the book you now hold in your hands.

The first thing that I learned was that it has traditionally been accepted, in New England at least, that women don't have, or shouldn't demonstrate, a sense of humor. Some even say that there is a stigma attached to being a funny woman. Think of the social gatherings you have attended over the years. Who usually tells the jokes? You got it.

Humor, like alcohol, seems to have been pretty much a sport for men, carried on in places "ladies" didn't frequent, like saloons, barber shops, smoking coaches and in the political arena. Women were admonished not to exercise their wit.

An 1842 issue of *Graham's Magazine* (for the genteel) stated:

> Women have sprightliness, cleverness, smartness, but little wit. There is a body and substance in true wit, with a reflectiveness rarely found apart from a masculine intellect . . . the female does not admit of it.

Forty years later, Kate Sanborn, writer and critic, insisted that it was only an "apparent lack" and offered the following explanation:

> Women do not find it politic to cultivate or express their wit. No man likes to have his story capped by a fresher and better from a lady's lips . . . No, no, it's dangerous, if not fatal.

There are many books concerning the history of American humor, but with the exception of Stephen Leacock's *Humor and Humanity,* 1938, female humorists aren't mentioned. Leacock praises Anita Loos for her *Gentlemen Prefer Blondes,* but only after announcing: "Women are not humorous except by exception." The humorous works of Emily Kimbrough, Cornelia Otis Skinner, Maine's own Fanny Fern, Elizabeth Stuart Phelps, and Sappho have been all but forgotten. Forgotten, too, is that period between 1900 and 1940 when the publishing field contained a plethora of women writing light, humorous fiction. Authors such as Nora Ephron *(Crazy Salad),* Fran Leibowitz *(Metropolitan Life),* and Margaret Atwood *(Lady Oracle)* are still writing humor in the 1980's.

In literature, funny women have been seen as distasteful. Jo, the main character in Louisa Mae Alcott's *Little Women,* was criticized by her sisters for her wit and for not being "feminine."

Although W. D. Howells, sympathetic to the suppression of female humor, intended in *The Rise of Silas Lapham* to give Penelope, the first fictional heroine with a sense of humor, full reign of her wit, he ended up portraying her as masculine and possessing a "lazy and drawling way with the vernacular." Eventually she was exiled to Mexico (just a male impersonator after all?).

With all of this information under my belt I charged off in

search of women with funny stories to tell. After a year and a half of advertising for works, and interviewing people across the state, I found myself with less than enough material to fill a thin book. They (the funny women) were in the woodwork, of that I was sure, for I had grown up with a wonderfully funny mother and had been bumping into witty women all of my life. Where were they hiding? Well, another year exposed them.

Writing humor isn't such an easy thing. As a matter of fact, it's very serious business. The imagination of the humorist is hard pressed to stay ahead of the surrealism of life. At times it seems that American life has become its own parody and satire and competes with the humorist. Perhaps not, but one wonders when hearing about the Georgian undertaker who opened the drive-up funeral parlor so that mourners could gear down and pay their respects. Then we hear about the prostitutes in New York who are threatening to unionize for better walking conditions.

Defining humor is even more difficult because it is different things to different people. E. B. White (male, but again Maine's own) once said that trying to define humor was a little like trying to perfect the craft of blowing bubbles: "It won't take much blowing up and it won't take much probing. It has a certain fragility, an evasiveness, which one had best respect."

Ladies' Choice is only the fourth collection of humor by American women to be published. In 1885, Kate Sanborn railed against *The Guide to Perfect Gentility* warning women against being humorous by publishing *Wit of Women.* Mary Beard published another anthology in the late Nineteenth Century. Deanne Stillman and Anne Beatts, of the television program "Saturday Night Live," edited *Titters* in 1976.

The humor in this anthology is not typically "Down East," although some pieces are definitely so flavored. It also includes a sharpness of wit and a satirical perspective on issues involving the "domestics." For instance, Catherine Burns' immediate response to raising three children alone is impending madness, but retrospectively viewed with a slightly humorous cant, she proposes a solution: making the Pill retroactive. Liz Albert writes about dog training and its disciplinary effect on the owner. When Brute snatches her steak and runs off to the living room, she establishes immediately who is boss. "Brute, does it need more salt?"

Hopefully *Ladies' Choice* will make you smile, laugh, and perhaps even groan.

Mavis Patterson
Editor

Liz Albert

BRINGING UP BRUTE

Yessir, the only way to handle a dog, large or small, is to be firm and consistent with him, while at the same time letting him know that you care. Some dog owners tend to be intimidated by their pets. This is unfortunate, for the dog soon senses your insecurity, and you will encounter resistance from him at every turn. You must let him know, gently but firmly, that *you* are the boss.

The other night, for example, as we sat down to a delicious steak dinner, Brute lunged at my plate and made off with my sirloin between his fangs. Not one to be daunted by this playful act, I quickly but calmly followed him into the living room where he was proceeding to devour my dinner on our new carpeting.

My approach was simple and direct, and clearly established who was Master. Clyde Beatty would have been proud. "Brute," I said firmly, "does it need more salt?"

Many dog owners participate in local obedience classes. Here again is an excellent opportunity to let your dog know where he stands. As you work together, jumping over hurdles and learning the basic commands, mutual feelings of respect and

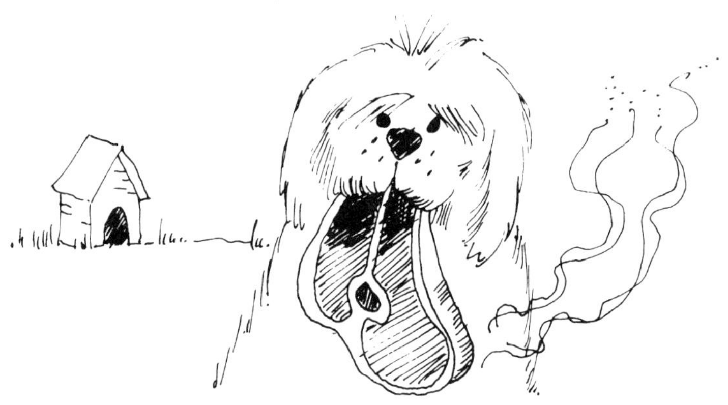

trust will undoubtedly develop. Brute is quite eager for his classes to begin next week. I do hope he'll be gentle with the choke chain, though. I have a rather sensitive neck.

The local Humane Society has been very kind and helpful to us throughout the raising of our pet, and their understanding and cooperation has been invaluable. They have even agreed to let us sleep over there on weekends when Brute decides that he wants the house to himself.

***Liz Albert** of Portland is married and is the Assistant Director of Pharoah's House, a halfway house for prisoners. She doesn't own a dog.*

Anonymous

A NEWFIE MOTHER WRITING TO HER SON

My dear Son –

Just a few lines to let you know that I am still alive. I am writing this letter slowly because I know you can't read fast. You won't know the house when you come home – we've moved. It was a lot of trouble moving. The most difficult thing was the bed. You see, the man wouldn't let us take it in the taxi. It wouldn't have been too bad if your father hadn't been sleeping in it at the time.

About your father – he has a lovely new job. He has 500 men under him. He's cutting the grass at the cemetery.

Your sister got herself engaged to that fellow she has been going out with. He gave her a beautiful ring with three stones missing.

Our neighbors, the Browns, started to keep pigs. We just got wind of it this morning. I got my appendix out and a dishwasher put in.

There was a washing machine in the house when we moved in but it isn't working too good. Last week I put in four shirts, pulled the chain, and I haven't seen the shirts since.

Your little brother came home from school yesterday. All the boys in his school have new suits. We can't afford to buy him a new one, but we are going to buy him a new hat and let him sit in the window.

Your sister, Mary, had a baby this morning. I haven't heard yet if it is a boy or a girl, so I don't know if you are an aunt or an uncle.

Your uncle Amos was drowned last week in a vat of whiskey in Dominion Brewery. Four of his workmates dived in to save him but he bravely fought them off. We cremated his body and it took three days to put out the fire.

Kate is now working in a mill at Grand Falls. She's been there now for six weeks. I'm sending her some clean underwear as she says she is on the same shift as when she started.

Your father didn't have much to drink at Christmas. I put a bottle of castor oil in his beer. It kept him going until New Year's day. I went to the doctor on Thursday. Your father came with me. The doctor put a small glass tube in my mouth and told me not to open it for ten minutes. Your father offered to buy it from him, but it was not for sale.

It only rained twice last week, first for three days and then for four. Monday was so windy that one hen laid the same egg four times.

We had a letter yesterday from the undertaker. He said that if the last installment isn't paid on your grandmother within seven days, up she comes.

I must close now, because the plumber is coming here to repair the pipes and there's a shocking smell.

Your Mother

P.S. I was going to send you ten dollars, but I have already sealed the envelope.

M. Catherine Burns

DR. SOCK

Today they finally did it to me. For years, I've battled the impending insanity which is every mother's constant bedfellow.

"Okay, Creeps," I said to them before I began to babble, "you've won. I give up. Which one of you took my eyeglasses? You? You? Or...? Oh, don't worry, Peter Perfect, I know *you'd* never do anything wrong." How can such evil, criminal little minds feel at home on such childishly innocent faces, I wonder.

Three unconvincing voices scream out in self-defense to tunes reminiscent of Watergate. "To the best of my recollection..." says one. "Aw, shut up!" I holler. "In *this* house you're all guilty till proven innocent. "That's Un-American!" protests a freckle-faced instigator. "Our social studies book says..." "Never mind your social studies book, my old catechism says all children are born with venial sin on their souls. And Dr. Sock says all kids are animals."

"Who's Dr. Sock?" they wonder.

"He's a Chinese child psychologist," I say through clenched teeth and gritted fists. "His full name is Dr. Sock-It-To-'Em and I'm just about ready to..." I wave a threatening fist under

their noses, trying to sound at least like Muhammed Ali's mother. "Cough up with them glasses, Whities. I am the greatest!"

It isn't working, I conclude. My approach is all wrong. I loom over them like a Not-So-Jolly Green Giant. Well, the book *says* to approach a problem from all angles. They back up a little and I realize I'm making some progress. I take another step forward and six little sneakers rhythmically back up another step. But they're still smirking. And behind one of those smirks is a pair of eyeglasses. I take a long, *swooping* step this time and they respond in kind. But they're still smirking and now one of them is humming.

"Who's HUMMING?" I demand.

"*I* am," says an eight-year-old boy wonder. "Hey, Mom, maybe this is how that Arthur Murray guy got started."

"Arthur Murray, my foot," I scream. "You want me to do the Bump on your nose? Or how about the Twist on your toes?"

"Hey, neato, that rhymes," says the poet laureate.

"This *isn't* finding out where my glasses are," I remind them.

"Your gwasses isn't in the toilet, Mommy," a three-year-old contributes. "*I* didn't fwush 'em down."

The room suddenly seems strange and far away. And there's a babbling lunatic sitting in the corner, speaking in a strange tongue. They finally did it to me. They nominated me for the Myopic-Mad-Mother-of-the-Year award. And I think I'll win it.

ON SURVIVING THREE SONS

"Congratulations! You have another son." Somewhere in the drugged consciousness of the post-natal period, these words echoed for the third time. And disbelief wormed its way through the news.

"Me? Have *another* son? But *nobody* has three boys!" I opened an eye slowly and consciously, and the perfect little creature before me looked back. Somehow the scene seemed peculiarly familiar, like a rerun of an old Sunday night movie.

The first thing I ever did with each of the three boys was to run a quick spot-check on them, minutes after their arrival. Who knows? Maybe the doctor was wrong. Or maybe God, knowing how desperately I wanted a daughter, had given me a hermaphrodite as a compromise. But no, they were 100% boy and I was destined to be their mother, all the way.

Each little crisis that I have survived only seems to make room for another, though. Like the War of the Pets.

"We have to have an animal, Mom," they decided.

"What! With three boys, I need more animals in this place?"

We tried a puppy first, but he got tired of Pepsi-Cola baths and being dressed in mis-matched pajamas. Sambo, the cat, joined us next. He'd been with us for three months and it began to look like this might work out. I overlooked it the time they sheared him and even the afternoon they baked his litter box in my new range. But one day a friend arrived and I started to serve coffee. As I reached into the refrigerator for milk, Sambo leaped out, shivering, and made a beeline for the front door. That was the last time we ever saw him. Herman was next. Even our little hamster was male, but I decided that mothering *him* would be easy since *he* came with a cage. The boys fed him sunflower seeds – in bed, naturally – and when Herman got bored in his three-foot cage, they let him loose. This little game was called Hide-and-Shriek because an unsuspecting mother made stupid screaming noises when she found him in the Saltine cracker box or in her hair dryer hose. I *know* they have another game, but nobody will admit to playing this one. It's called Let's Drive Mommy Bonkers and it's played in rotating eight-hour shifts, 'round the clock.

I have a few of my own amusements, too, that I keep to myself... like tempting little thoughts that raced through my head when I was ready to leave on a long journey and discovered one son missing. Like a fool, I searched for him, and found him packed away in the very front of a U-Haul trailer. To further testify to my insanity, I only spent five minutes enjoying all the blissful possibilities before letting him out.

Through all the years, however, I've been fortunate in having an excellent hobby to divert what's left of my mind. I have done years of earnest research on a method of making the Pill retroactive. The project is nearing a significant breakthrough and I find myself grinning even more these days.

TO COOK OR NOT TO COOK

A few years ago, Peg Bracken published a book called *The I Hate To Cook Book.* In sincere sympathy to her views, I am ready to publish a sequel called *I'll Die Trying.* Though cooking is my Achille's heel, I know I can, with extreme effort, put *something* in my mouth besides my foot.

Psychology plays an important role in my attempts. Today, for example, I took the time to serve the children an appetizer. It didn't work. They knew it was last night's hot dogs, dressed up in Monday's leftover cheese. I didn't get discouraged, though. After burning both elbows removing an Ebony Casserole from the oven, I said cheerily, "Now here's something else to whet your appetites."

A little voice translated, "She means we'll have to wash it down."

"Knock it off," I warn, "you know Mama tries."

"Why can't we have a Big Mac instead?" an emaciated eight-year-old begs. In our home, you see, we give McDonald's such a volume of business that they deliver to us in plain, brown wrappers.

"Forget McDonald's – I'm the boss in the kitchen."

A second voice corrects, "You mean you're lost in the kitchen." I chose to ignore that one.

"What's this stuff?" another asks, holding up a black, crusted cube.

"That's French croquettes, a la charcoal," I say defensively.

"French croquettes!" the detective hollers. "How come everything that looks burned is called French? French toast, French hot dogs, French sauerkraut."

"Look," I say convincingly, "it's a proven fact that charcoal is good for the digestive tract."

My children, you see, are cursed with a tact that carries with it more potential destruction than anything *I* could ever cook. In addition, they are name droppers.

"Why can't we just have raw hickory nuts?" one begs. "Euell Gibbons eats them."

"Euell Gibbons," I say with a threatening glare, "stalked wild asparagus, too. Does that mean we have to?"

"Well, why can't you fix something like the Galloping Gourmet makes?"

"Because," I scream, "the Galloping Gourmet is nothing but a jockey with a food fetish. Now start eating!"

Three little heads bow in reverent prayer. "Bless us, O Lord, and these, Thy gifts, which we are about to regret..."

"Cut it out!" I warn. "A lot of kids in China are going hungry right at this very moment."

"What a way to go!" one says enviously.

My poor ego suffers so much damage in the kitchen that I'm ready to throw in the towel. But tonight I decided to make a final effort.

"I'm going to bake a pie for you children."

"What's a pie?" one wonders.

"Those are the things you see pictures of in magazines, remember?" the smart aleck informs him.

"Shut up," I say, "before I put all of you on Dr. Stillman's water diet permanently!" I can't deny, however, the fact that diet *does* play an important role. And today I saw another book. This one was called *You Are What You Eat.* My God, are we in trouble!

***M. Catherine Burns** lives in Waterville with her three children, and works for Keyes Fibre there. She writes poetry, humor, and lyrics.*

Joyce Butler

NONSENSE

The world is too much with me; I've begun to talk nonsense again. Did I say again? I never really stopped. But when I get too busy and preoccupied and tired I talk more nonsense than usual. Yesterday, after hearing the children tell about a fun happening at school, I said, "Oh, I wish I'd been a mouse on the wall." The children registered only brief surprise and made no comment; they've come to expect such remarks from me. But I visualized in my mind's eye a mouse clinging precariously to a wall while straining to look over his shoulder at the happenings below, and I had a private chuckle for myself.

The children and I learned long ago that I have a private little vocabulary of my own. We discovered that when I say "maybe" I mean "yes," that "I'll think about it" means "probably," that a quick "no" usually means "I'll think about it," and "I doubt it" means "no." This translation is fairly standard, and we take it in stride. But translating nonsense is a little more difficult. A remark like, "Put the door out and close the cat" is easily understood, but when I'm really preoccupied I say some startling things. One day I surprised Leslie by telling her, "I'm going to eat you at 5 o'clock." What I meant was, "Supper is

at five." Jamie had a little trouble deciphering, "Put your feet on," but of course soon realized that I was saying, "Put your shoes on." And even I had to stop and think when I told Stephanie, "If you practice your homework before you write your piano then you'll be ready for bed before you go to school." Actually we never did figure that one out.

I suppose it isn't serious that I have this weakness. Actually we all find it rather interesting when I say at breakfast, "Hurry up and drink your dinner or you'll miss the bus," but I'm a little worried because I'm afraid my weakness may be catching. The other afternoon Jamie, who was on his way out to play, called from the doorway, "Goodnight, Mama."

"Goodnight," I answered cheerfully. He stopped in surprise and listened back to hear what he had said and then grinned and said, "Mama, you know what I mean."

If Jamie has picked up my inclination to talk nonsense that means the rest of the family could, too. Five people talking nonsense could make for a chaotic household. I don't think we've got time for that much nonsense; we are busy people. But then again, maybe we'd have so much fun we wouldn't have time to be busy . . . or something like that.

***Joyce Butler** of Kennebunk is married and has three children. She works for the Brick Stove Museum in Kennebunk.*

Rebecca S. Cummings

KNIT ONE

I threw the old purple sweater over my shoulders and slipped on the plaid oven mitts, a Christmas present from the boys. Carefully, I carried the still-steaming apple pie across the fresh snow to Fred's. His house was a little two-room camp, but Fred said it was enough for him, and he could keep it nice and warm with the wood cookstove. And for an old man living alone, it was easy enough to keep clean. The snow squeaked underfoot. Sticky juice dribbled over the edge of the pie, staining the new mitt.

A jay sassed loudly from the hemlock behind the woodshed, and snow flurried down from the branches. I had to squint in the bright sun, but I saw the jay, as blue as the sky, swoop down and pick up a crust of bread. Fred must have put out scraps for the birds. He often did.

"Fred!" I called. "Fred, open up!" My breath made little clouds now that I was standing in the shade, and I was regretting not having put on more than the sweater. "Fred! Are you there?"

"Come on in, Liz'beth. Door's always open." His voice was muffled from inside.

"Can't! My hands are full!" I hollered.

"Well, hold your horses then, girl." I could feel his step coming across the floor.

"Mornin', Liz," he said as he opened the door. He moved aside so I could pass through. "Huh? What you got there?"

"Apple pie. Right out of the oven." I set the pie on a pile of newspapers on the pitted table.

"Smells awful good. You sure are good to a neighbor, Liz'beth. You goin' to stop for a minute? Maybe have a little coffee?"

"No coffee, but I will visit for a few minutes." I sat down in one of the two kitchen chairs. "I left some stuff in the dryer and it'll be ready before long." Fred settled into the blackened oak rocker.

It was as neat as a pin in the little room. The cot, that was also a couch, was made up, covered with a ribbed tan spread that had once been on Bobby's bed. A few dishes, none of them matching, were stacked in the dish drainer. It smelled of beans baking, a Saturday smell. A geranium with a brilliant new bloom basked in the warm sunshine of the windowsill. The clock, a fine old Seth Thomas, on the shelf above the refrigerator chimed the half hour and then continued its ticking, setting the pace for Fred's rocking. Fred picked up the knitting that he had been working on before I came.

"What are you making now?" I asked.

"Mittens. For your Timmy." He held up the tubular piece and I could see the growing cuff, bright red with a green stripe. "When I get through with these, I'll make some for Bobby. Diff'rent color maybe."

"Timmy will like those. You make the best mittens the kids have all winter. They keep their hands so nice and warm."

"Kids need mittens," he said.

I watched, fascinated by his big gnarled fingers, knobby from arthritis, manipulating the four needles and the long swirl of yarn. “Fred, how’d you ever learn to knit? I never knew a man who could knit before.”

“No . . . I wouldn’t suppose you have.” He looked up from his work. His eyes twinkled. “Now, if you really want to know, take yourself a little coffee from that pot and I’ll tell you.”

I took a clean cup from the dish drainer and poured half a cup of the strong coffee that had been sitting on a wire rack at the back of the stove. I helped myself to milk from the refrigerator, the old kind with rounded corners. “Sure you don’t want some, too?” I asked him.

“Nope. Had enough already.”

I sipped at the coffee and went back for more milk. “Whew!” I said, trying to hold back the grimace. “You sure make a strong brew!”

“Keeps a person awake.”

“Okay, Fred. Now tell me.”

He clacked his teeth and sighed, readying himself. The chair creaked. The clock ticked, taking us back.

It was winter . . . Feb’uary, I think. Yes . . . it was Feb’uary. We had one of the worst snows ever that year. Course we didn’t have no plows in them days, and it made it seem all the worse to do all that clearin’ by hand.

Mother was fit to be tied when she got that letter sayin’ her sister Clara down in Roxbury in Mass’chusetts was dyin’. She wanted to go down there to be with her somethin’ awful. ’Course, it bein’ winter, it weren’t the easiest thing. And then there was the four of us. I was only . . . let me see . . . thirteen, I’d say. Mina was a year older, and Frank . . . Frank musta been sixteen. And Floyd, he woulda been seventeen. Mother was pretty unsure about leavin’ us and goin’ off in the dead of winter, but Father decided her on it, and he even went with her.

I got to go along with Floyd when he took them with the

team and sledge to the train station. It was some cold that winter. Mother cried all the way to the train, worryin' about Aunt Clara and worryin' about leavin' us and the cold and maybe fires. Father kept tellin' her Floyd was old enough to take care of the farm and even I, as puny as I was then, could be a big help to him. Nevertheless, she cried, full of worries I suppose, and kissed us good-bye. Father shook our hands and reminded us to go to church on Sunday and to get the chores done reg'lar.

We watched the train pull out of Market Square, and we waved until all we could see was the caboose. It was funny for me goin' home without them – they'd never been away before, at least not as I could remember – and it musta been for Floyd too 'cause he didn't talk none at all. Those two big work horses, Tom and Molly their names was, seemed to go right along with such a light load, the two of us nothin' but boys. Well, Mina had some dinner for us and we ate – I remember how quiet it was – and then we loafed around all afternoon until it was time to do the night chores.

Frank and Floyd did most of the milkin' and I cleaned up under the cows and tended to the hens and turkeys. We had six turkeys then. The first ones we'd ever had. Mother had wanted to try some turkeys and she'd begged and begged Father to let her have some. He got her six of 'em, and she took care of 'em herself every day. They was in their own separate part of the hen house. Great big things beside them hens.

The next day bein' Sunday, we hitched up the team and went to church. Seems everyone already knew about Aunt Clara, and all the women, especially, felt sorry for us kids. 'Course we boys knew enough to look down and out. We was invited to three diff'rent houses for Sunday dinner. Frank decided we'd go to Pike's. He knew they'd have a big ham and maybe a puddin' for dessert and, sure enough, they did.

Mina and I was still in school then. On Monday mornin' she

hurried us through breakfast and did the dishes and swept up. Floyd and Frank went into the woods, but Mina and I walked the mile and a half or so – you see, there was no school buses then – to the Clark School. Miss Witham was the teacher. If I close my eyes I can still see that woman. She had some temper. There was a bunch of Finn kids in the school, and when they'd start talkin' Finn, she never knew a word they said. I even learned a few words so I could talk pretty good with 'em, too. She got real sore when we did. 'Course she didn't know what was goin' on. Then she made a rule we could only talk in English.

One time she got mad at Carl Wouri and me. Can't remember now what for. Maybe we was talkin' Finn or we had a dead squirrel or somethin', like boys do. Anyway, she chased us right out to the pine trees. Then we got scared she'd tell our folks, so we let her catch us and give us a strappin'. Mina was good in school, real good at rememberin' things, and Miss Witham liked Mina. She sometimes gave her little pieces of candy wrapped up in fancy papers. 'Course Mina shared.

I remember how dark it was that Monday. We knew a big one was comin'. It was snowin' pretty hard that afternoon when we was goin' home, and the wind was beginnin' to pick up. And was it ever cold! We was about froze when we got home. Floyd and Frank weren't back from the woods yet, and Mina fretted, just like Mother, but they finally got back. By that time, we'd got the fires all goin' again and the house was warmin' up.

All night we heard the wind howlin'. The cold came right in around the windows and in any little crack. And the woodshed was fillin' up with snow. Floyd slept on the little couch, more like a bench, and kept the fires goin'. He prob'ly didn't sleep none too good that night. The next mornin' we could see we was pretty well snowed in. It took us a heck of a while to shovel a little path to the barn, but we got them cows milked.

We didn't bother tryin' to take the milk to the corner where it usually got picked up for town, we just put them cans in the milk house. Mina and I didn't go to school that day.

So we boys stayed inside and played checkers and cribbage, and my job was to keep the woodbox full. Mina was knittin' on somethin' and she did some cookin' and she kept sputterin' about havin' to clean up the water on the floor that came in on our boots every time we'd go out to check on the snow. All day long it kept up. The wind blew like a son-uv-a-gun, and sometimes we thought for sure the roof was goin' to end up on t'other side of the mountain.

The next day it wasn't snowin' so hard, but the wind was still blowin' and it had gotten a lot colder. We kept the lamps burnin' most of the day, the snow was drifted up so high against the windows. It was that dark inside. Again we played cribbage and checkers, but we was gettin' a little bored and fit to be tied at bein' so cooped up.

Then in the afternoon, Floyd, he went down cellar and came back up with a big coffee mug full of Father's cider. Father kept cider back then. He said since he was man enough to take care of the farm and us, he was man enough to have a little of that cider.

Well, pretty soon Frank thought he'd have a little too, to keep Floyd company. Mina didn't like it none and she told Frank and Floyd to keep right out of it, but they didn't listen to her. Then Frank asked me, didn't I want a swig? Now, I'd tasted cider before and didn't much like it, but 'course I didn't tell that to Frank and Floyd. I was feelin' pretty big, goin' down cellar with 'em. Well, you can guess what happened. We three got drunk, roarin', snortin' drunk.

Somehow that night we got the cows milked. I guess doin' the chores was so automatic we could do it no matter how we was. Frank got kicked in the leg, but he didn't even know it 'til the next day when he had a big bruise on his shin, and we figured that's what happened.

We'd taken some of that cider to the barn with us in two cannin' jars, and after we finished the milkin' we took a couple more swigs each. Then Floyd remembered the hens and turkeys; we'd near forgotten 'bout 'em, so I went to do that. The turkeys was out of water. What little they had was all froze up. I was on my way to get some, but Floyd said to wait. He had an idea.

Then he poured the rest of that cider outa one of them jars into the water dish. Those turkeys musta been some thirsty 'cause they come right over, gabblin' like they do, and they just drunk right up. We was kinda curious 'bout how they'd behave, so we stood around and watched. Let me tell you, they liked that cider! And sure enough, they got to wobblin' 'bout the same as us. Now we thought that was real funny. We kept at it, right along with 'em, drinkin' and hootin' and hollerin'.

Well, it didn't take long. First one fell over and then another and then another. We got a little scared. We figured they was all dyin'. Mina would find out, which would be bad enough – she being like a little mother with all her rules – but Mother and Father was bound to be home sometime soon and then we'd get it for sure. We tried to think what to do. We thought we could leave 'em there and pretend they froze, but that didn't seem so good.

Then Frank, he says since they was dead anyways, we ought to pluck 'em and they'd at least be ready for the stew pot and maybe Mina, for one, wouldn't be so sore. So we each grabbed one and started pluckin' them feathers out. What a nasty job that was.

Floyd and Frank was pretty fast, and they finished their first ones and started their second ones. Bein' so much younger, I was a lot slower. Then I noticed that the one I was workin' on maybe wasn't so dead after all. It moved around some. I told Frank and Floyd and we checked 'em all over and sure enough, they wasn't dead. But they might as well have been, all them feathers picked off so they was near bare-assed naked.

We musta been in the barn pretty long, cause Mina, mad as she was at us, comes in lookin' for us. You shoulda seen her when she sees them turkeys! She hollered b'Jesus and told us to spend the night in the barn. She went back and got a blanket and took each one of them birds all wrapped up into the kitchen. So them turkeys, dead drunk and hardly a feather left on 'em, spent the night in the kitchen next to the stove, and we boys slept in the barn. 'Course we buried ourselves in the hay and that kept us pretty warm.

It seemed the next mornin' that the storm outside was pretty near over, but inside me it was just startin'. I puked for a while down the gutter and that made me feel a little better. I wasn't the only one, though. When we got through, we headed for the kitchen together. Mina was right there. She had fire in her eyes. Those turkeys was all still alive, but they was huddled together, and we knew that if we put 'em in the pen they'd freeze for sure, but we couldn't keep 'em in the kitchen either. Already the floor was a mess.

Mina made all three of us sit down on the kitchen bench and without even gettin' us any breakfast, she got out knittin' needles and balls of scrap yarn and showed us how to knit. 'Course we weren't in no position to argue with her. She could be pretty willful when she put her mind to it, even back then. The four of us knit all mornin' and into the afternoon and we made five little coats. Well, more like vests, all diff'rent colors – brown and green and some had blue on 'em and yellow. They weren't none too beautiful, lots of holes and lumps, but we tied 'em around those turkeys.

We had to fix up a box in the kitchen for 'em. They hopped around in those little shirts and, believe it or not, four of 'em made it. One died sometime that afternoon, but four of 'em made it. And 'course there was the lucky one that just had a

headache like us, but at least it still had its feathers. Thanks to me for bein' so slow at pluckin'.

That night we boys was still feelin' poorly and we went to bed early. The next day we shoveled pretty near the whole day. We did our chores up just like they was supposed to be done. Floyd and Frank finally went back to the woods. Mina and I went back to school. We got the place all spic an' span so it looked real good by the time Mother and Father come home four days later. Aunt Clara had died.

When Mother saw her turkeys, she cried and cried. She said her boys was all headed down the wrong path. She wouldn't speak at all to Floyd and Frank. I was the one got the worst of it. She hugged me real tight 'gainst her bosom and prayed and prayed for me. Father just strapped the three of us.

The hour chimed. The clock ticked on.

His needles clicked. He was working the opening for the thumb.

"So that's when I learned to knit. Kinda liked it and been doin' it now and again ever since. Made me two, three sweaters. Still have one."

Laughing, I pushed aside the coffee I hadn't drunk. "Fred Strout, I never know whether to believe you or not! But I know my Timmy will be able to use another pair of mittens."

I gave him a kiss on his prickly cheek before dashing off to take my clothes out of the dryer.

Rebecca S. Cummings *submitted her story after reading about* Ladies' Choice *in the local media. She lives in Wells.*

Rachel Elaine Day

IS THERE AN AUTHOR IN THE HOUSE?

I envy couples who each evening have stimulating conversations in tidy, picture perfect homes. My husband returns to a house each night that looks like grenades have been thrown in every room. It's no wonder his favorite pastime is the television screen.

"I'm going to write a story about your mother," I said after I had tucked the children into bed.

"Mmmmm, that's nice," he mumbled. Walter liked to be consulted on important matters. The most advantageous time to do this is while he is watching the reruns of his favorite commercials. Last week he consented to buy a new living room set, complete service for sixteen in English bone china, and my spring wardrobe during the Playtex living bra advertisement.

The next day trouble began.

"Hey Dad," my oldest son, Jeff, said. "Mom's writing some neat stuff about Grandma." I knew he was into the snooping stage, but up to now I had nothing to hide except possibly my bust development course and a children's sex education book that deserved an X rating.

"Me and the guys had a blast reading all that junk laying

around on the ironing board," he said excitedly. I hadn't realized that at age twelve he had turned into a stoolie. I stuffed a dirty paper towel into his mouth, but it was too late.

"You wouldn't," my husband moaned. "You couldn't..."

"Why not? She's a real character. Besides, she deserves it."

"Doesn't the sake of family mean anything to you?" he asked with feeling. "Is nothing sacred? If she finds out you're writing about her she probably won't speak to you for a year."

"That would be one way to get a little peace," I said hopefully.

"Can't you write about television?" he pleaded.

"How about the way she marches up and changes the channel in the middle of my favorite show so that she can watch Lawrence Welk?" I replied. "She doesn't even ask."

"That's not what I had in mind. Why don't you write about laundry detergents?" he said sarcastically.

"Sure. Remember the time the soap company interviewed her, coast to coast? She told them she tried to convince me to use their product because the kids' diapers looked like I washed the cellar floor with them. She even gave my name and address over the air. Cars with out of state housewives drove by for months to see the dingy things hanging on the line. She made me famous."

"You're exaggerating," he said.

"No, I'm not. What about the time she threw up at the church supper?"

"What about it? She had a touch of the flu. It could happen to anybody."

"Yes I know," I replied. "But she didn't have to announce to two hundred people that it was my casserole that had made her sick. Do you realize that in the past four years the dinner committee has only let me bring butter? Even the Cub Scout den mother asked me to bring olives to the last banquet. Word gets around you know."

"You're being over sensitive," he said.

"Oh yeah? Then how come the kids came home from Sunday School last week and asked what botulism was?" I wailed. "I'll bet they didn't find that word in the Bible."

"Now don't you get upset. Why don't you think up a little article on housework? On second thought, maybe you'd better write about something you've had more experience with," he said as he cautiously looked around.

"Even you are against me," I cried. "You should have taken your mother's advice and married the girl she chose for you, the one who irons her husband's socks."

"Well," he said, "she obviously knows what an ironing board is for. Why you use it for a desk is beyond me."

"I just figured I should put that skinny thing with legs to some use," I murmured darkly. "Is that what that thing is?"

"In all our years of wedded bliss, have you ever turned on the iron?" he demanded.

"What's an iron?"

"You're impossible," he said.

"Don't change the subject. Do you realize that when your mother comes to visit, she always sniffs my stove fan looking for odors?" I complained. "She told me once that she thought the mice had their cemetery up there in the vent. Last week she told me I should keep the litter box cleaner, and she knows we don't own a cat. I told her the fumes came from the dirty socks *she* taught you to stash under the bed."

"You're being ridiculous," he said.

"Well, why is it at any gathering, I can always depend on her to pat you on the shoulder and call you 'poor boy' and hug the kids and call them 'Grandma's little waifs'?"

"That's her form of endearment," he justified. "Besides, I doubt you could find enough material to write a very interesting story about her."

"Are you kidding? I could go on for volumes – maybe make

it a new division on the Book of the Month Club," I answered. "How many other grandmothers do you know that set children under a bright light for hours at a stretch to grill them when they visit her? 'Does Mommy have strange men call her? How much did her new dress cost?' The kids are starting to complain."

"OK, OK, you may have a point. But this time I insist; I put my foot down. I absolutely forbid you to write about my mother!! Your little hobby has gone too far," he roared as he stormed out of the room.

It was all out in the open now. I'd suspected for a long time that he thought of my writing as a strange personality trait and not anything to be taken seriously. Now my suspicions were confirmed.

"You think so, huh?" I gasped to myself. "My LITTLE HOBBY? Someday, you're going to get paid back for that statement." At that moment the phone rang. With delicious pleasure I passed the call from Grandma on to her beloved son, who was settling into his favorite chair to watch T.V.

"Um, uh huh, um, ah, no, yes, well, OK," he yawned. Twenty minutes later he hung up and came into the kitchen.

"That sounded like a brilliant conversation," I said. "What did she have to say?"

"Nothing much, but she needs some eggs, and asked if I'd get some for her," he said as he put on his coat.

"It's hard to believe that's all she said in twenty minutes. She lives just around the corner from the store. Did she break her leg today? How come she can't drive her own car to get them?" I questioned.

"She had her car washed today and doesn't want to get the tires dirty," he said. "She talks so fast that I'd agreed to shop for her before I realized it. Anyway, it will only take a few minutes and it won't hurt to humor her a bit. Hold dinner; I'll be back soon."

Two hours later, he wearily plodded through the door.

"You won't believe what I've been through," he complained.

"If it involves your mother, I'd believe anything. What took you so long?"

"I picked up the eggs and took them back to her house. Then she asked me to nail down a couple of boards on the back porch," he said. "Then, I returned a picnic basket to Aunt Sarah that she had left at Mother's last summer, and Aunt Sarah gave me a jar of pickles to take back to Mother. When I took the pickles back she decided she needed a prescription filled, immediately, so I made a trip to the pharmacy and went back to the house with that. Just as I was about to leave, she asked me to check the fuse box because the kitchen light wasn't working right. Of course it needed a new fuse, and of course she didn't have one. So I had to go to the store again."

"Sounds like a lot of fun," I said smugly. "You've accomplished quite a lot since you left here."

"That's not all," he said. "After I put the fuse in and was backing out the door, she put six boxes of candy that her club is selling in my arms. She had called her friends while I was at the store and told them I would deliver the candy right away. Now I have twelve dollars in my pocket to pay for the candy and I don't dare take it to her. I might never get home again."

"Mail it to her," I said cheerfully. "That's the safest way."

"As far as I'm concerned, that's the only way," he muttered as he walked into the other room. "Where's the big yellow pad of paper I bought you the other day?"

"What on earth do you want to do with a pad of paper?" I questioned.

"I think I'll sit down at the ironing board and write a story about my mother."

***Rachel Elaine Day** of Winslow is married and the mother of three. She is the Director of Volunteers at the Osteopathic Hospital in Waterville, and writes for her own amusement.*

Cheryl Haynes

WALTER BUYS A STOVE

I was just settling in for a long, quiet weekend Saturday morning when Bob Collins' big green pickup pulled into my front yard. Bob was driving, and Walter was sitting on the passenger side.

"Good morning, Bob," I said. "Good morning, Walter."

"Good nothing," Bob replied.

Walter said, "Stole my stove – ought to be hung."

"What?" I replied. "Stole your stove? Who?"

"If we knew who, we wouldn't have a problem," Bob retorted.

"Wait, back up a minute," I pleaded. "Someone stole Walter's stove?"

"Damn right," Bob said. "Took it right out of the kitchen, left the stovepipe lying in the entry way, soot and ashes all over the parlor rug. Just ripped it out and skedaddled with it."

"The old Atlantic Queen range, with the double oven, and the fancy scroll work across the back, and the eagle-claw feet?" I asked, incredulous. "Why, that's terrible."

"Damn right it is," Bob said.

"Stole my stove," said Walter. "Ought to be hung."

"So we're going up to Bangor to buy another stove," Bob

said. "Hop in the back."

"But, why do you want me to come?"

"Thought we might run into one of those fancy-talking salesmen, and you can translate for us."

I couldn't argue with that, so I hopped in the back of the pickup. The ride to Bangor was about as pleasant as an hour in a blast furnace, but we arrived without incident. Bob pulled up in front of a store that said "Post-Industrial Domestic Systems, Inc." I looked at the window display of composting toilets and turned to Bob.

"Are you sure this is the place you want to go?"

"Enid recommended it – she said they have the latest things in wood stoves." Enid is Bob's sister. She raises organic orchids, reads the *Maine Times,* and is considered something of a free-thinker within the family.

"Well," I said, "here goes nothing." We went in.

We were greeted at the door by a young man in Levi's and a T-shirt that read "Burn peat, not petro-dollars."

"Hi," he said, "my name is Jeff. Can I help you folks with something?"

"Ah, this is Bob," I said. "And this is Walter. They're looking for a woodstove."

"Stole my stove – ought to be hung," Walter muttered under his breath. Jeff looked at him sideways but decided to let it pass. "Fine, fine, we have a very fine selection here." He led us past gleaming rows of Jotuls, Fishers, Morsos and Ashleys.

"Now here's a beauty," Jeff said. "All sand-cast iron, firebrick lining, thermostatically controlled, burns in either the horizontal mode like a Franklin or in the vertical mode like an airtight, holds a fire for thirty-six hours, and the decorative tiles are removable, in case you want to change your color scheme..."

"Does it put out the cat?" Bob asked.

"I beg your pardon?" said Jeff.

"It does every other fool thing in creation – does it put out the cat?"

"Ah – no," Jeff said, "but the adjustable cooking top is removable for easy cleaning. And this side vent can be attached to your passive solar greenhouse, or vented right into your composting toilet. A terrific energy saver."

"I don't know," said Bob. "Walter's composting toilet is a good hundred feet from the house. How much does this monstrosity cost?"

"Only twelve thousand, nine hundred fifty-nine dollars, delivered and assembled," Jeff said. "Of course your pipe and venting would be more – probably about fifteen thousand dollars total."

"Godfrey Daniel," Bob said. "Walter's whole house ain't worth that, even throwing in the parlor rug and bed linens. You got anything cheaper?"

"Cheaper," said Jeff, "let's see . . . yes, now, this model is our basic utilitarian stove. All cast iron, with a lined firebox, inverted baffle system and heat exchanger, front and top loading, removable cooking top. It's airtight, holds a fire for eighteen hours, and it's only nine hundred and forty five dollars, including tax and delivery. And it comes in blue, red, or green enamel."

"What we going to do with the stove blacking?" Bob said.

"Stove blacking?" Jeff queried.

"Hades, yes," Bob said. "Walter won a lifetime supply of stove blacking from the Wormwood Stove and Fuel Company back in 1927. He ain't used but half of it."

"Oh, I see," said Jeff. "You want something with the traditional look – Early American, perhaps."

"I'm feeling earlier all the time," Bob replied.

"Step this way. I'm sure this is just what you're looking for." Jeff led the way down one aisle and across another. We all followed dutifully behind, Bob shaking his head, and Walter muttering, "Stole my stove – ought to be hung," and me trying to look like I was just an unattached browser among forests of andirons and meadows of Sod-o-lets.

"This is really our simplest stove," Jeff announced, making it clear that simple was synonymous with cheap. "It has your basic black finish, all cast iron, of course, with the fire-brick lining so you can burn either wood or coal, top or side loading. The over-sized firebox will take three-foot logs, and it will hold a fire for twelve hours. Only five ninety five."

"Perhaps I should explain . . ." I began.

"No," said Bob, "let me. You see, what we're looking for is a stove – a metal box you can put wood in and burn."

"Yes, sir, that's what we sell," said Jeff.

"No," said Bob, "seems to me what you sell is frills. Now, what's the point of having a stove that will hold a fire for six weeks?"

"Twelve hours," Jeff corrected. "I'm sure you wouldn't want to settle for less. With this stove you can go away and leave it all day, and you don't have to worry about your plants dying or your pipes freezing."

"I ain't got no plants," Walter spoke up. "And I ain't got no pipes. And there ain't no place I want to be for twelve hours at a stretch, except home, stoking the stove."

"Well," said Jeff, "then how about at night? With this stove, you'll still have a good bed of coals in the morning. That way, you don't have to build a new fire every day, just stir up the coals and put on some more wood."

"Young man," said Walter, "I've been building a new fire every morning for sixty two years. I wouldn't start the day with a leftover fire any more than I would eat breakfast off of last night's dirty dishes."

"But, sir," said Jeff, "a stove like this will hold its value. Why, in ten years you'll be able to sell it for more than you pay now."

"I don't want a damn investment," Walter said. "What I want is a damn stove."

"Ah, excuse me," I interrupted, "perhaps you have some used stoves we could look at? Something more along the lines of what my friend is used to?"

"Certainly," said Jeff. "Why didn't you say so?" He led the way to a dimly-lit back room that was crammed with rusty Franklins, pot-bellies and kitchen ranges. Bob and Walter picked their way among the wares, opening a door here, lifting a lid there. Suddenly, they came to a full stop. "Godfrey Daniels," Bob whispered. There in the half-light, its enamel gleaming softly, stood the Atlantic Queen range with the double oven, and the fancy scroll work across the back, and the eagle-claw feet. The store room was silent for a full minute, then Walter shouted, "Stole my stove – ought to be hung!"

"What?" said Jeff, his eyes bulging in the gloom. "Your stove? There must be some mistake. One of our suppliers brought this stove in just this morning. He's a very reliable man. I'm sure there's some mistake."

"Damn right there is," Bob said. "The mistake was in stealing a monogrammed stove. See the scroll work on the back – see them letters 'WLW'? Them's Walter's initials. The Atlantic Queen people made that stove up special for him back in 1927. You wait here, Walter. I'll get the truck."

Bob backed the pickup up to the loading dock, and he and Walter muscled the stove into it, with the help of a subdued and apologetic Jeff. He even gave Walter some new stovepipe free. When we got back to Walter's house, Walter and Bob and Bob's boy Luther got the stove re-installed in the kitchen, complete with the shiny new stovepipe. And that afternoon Enid came over and cleaned the soot off the parlor rug.

"It's the least I could do under the circumstances," she said.

"You're goddamn right," Bob replied.

WALTER GETS A LETTER

I was just sitting down to my second cup of coffee Saturday morning when Luther knocked on my kitchen door. Luther is Bob Collins' boy, which makes him Walter's grandnephew, on his father's mother's side. Luther had graduated from high school in June and started pumping gas at the corner store.

"Good morning, Luther," I said.

"Morning," said Luther, looking down at his shoes.

"Nice day," I added.

"Yes," said Luther, inspecting his right instep. Luther's on the shy side. He's a good boy – earnest, hard-working, reliable – but he'd make Calvin Coolidge sound like an auctioneer. As his father says, "Shy? That boy has got to be the shiest. When he got that job down to the store, I told him, 'Luther, now you're a working man, you've got to get some new shoes, ones with the Gettysburg Address printed on the toes, so you'll have something to read while you're looking at your feet.' "

"What can I do for you, Luther?" I asked. "Come in, have a cup of coffee."

"No, thanks. Walter wants you."

"What is it? Something wrong?"

"Don't know. He got a letter."

I knew it was useless to question Luther any further. I dumped my coffee down the sink and latched the screen door, and we climbed into Luther's rickety pick-up truck and drove out to Walter's house.

Luther chased the chickens and ducks out of the dooryard, and I picked my way through the used plumbing fixtures and over the lumber pile to the front door. Walter never throws anything away, at least not since his wife Edith died in 1952. Some say she drove herself to an early grave by trying to neaten up after Walter.

We found Walter in the front parlor. He was studying a piece of paper and muttering to himself. I cleared a month's accumulation of newspapers off the horsehair sofa and sat down. Luther stood near the door, shifting from one foot to the other.

"Good morning, Walter," I said. "Luther said you wanted to see me."

"Yes," said Walter. "Yes, I did. What do you make of that?" And he handed me the paper.

It was a letter from the town office, on official town stationery with the town seal at the top. The town seal shows a cow standing up to her knees in water, with a fish of undetermined species leaping over her back. A wreath of clams surrounds this tableau, with the words "Et aqua et terra profluent cum cena." It was designed in 1872 by Oren Tilden, then town poet, to commemorate the town's two chief industries, dairying and fishing. Oren's last direct descendant is Jake Tilden, who keeps the town dump.

The letter began, "Yes, the outward appearance of a person's property is important." It went on to say that the town selectmen had noticed an unsightly gathering of junk cars and general clutter in Walter's yard and would he please clean it up. It concluded by thanking Walter in advance for his cooperation, if any.

"Well?" said Walter.

"I guess they want you to clean up your yard," I said. "It's nothing personal. They sent out a couple dozen of these to people all over town."

"Clean up my yard?" said Walter. "What are they getting at? What's this mean, 'junk cars and general clutter'?"

"Well," I said, "I'm not sure—"

"You come out here in the yard and show me what they mean," Walter said. We adjourned to the yard, with Luther tagging along behind.

"Well?" said Walter.

"As for the junk cars," I said, "I guess they'd mean that pick-up, and the old Chevy there, and probably that station wagon, too." The pick-up was a rusty Ford with the back cut off and a wooden platform bolted to the frame. It was jacked up on cement blocks and the wheels were gone. The Chevy was an aging sedan, with four or five different shades of primer on the body and most of the windows missing. The station wagon, what was left of it, reposed beneath an ancient apple tree. The doors, hood, seats, wheels and most of the engine were gone.

"That pick-up," said Walter, "is my sugaring truck. Only use it to collect the sap in the spring. Got it jacked up so I can use the wheels on my farm truck. Ain't that right, Luther?"

"Yes," said Luther.

"And the Chevy," said Walter, "now, that's a classic. We're

restoring it, Luther and I. Ain't we, Luther?"

"Yes," said Luther.

"And the station wagon," said Walter, "is my parts car. Got to have a parts car. Everybody knows that."

"Yes, sir," said Luther, without being prompted.

"Well," I said, "I guess that takes care of the junk cars."

"I should say so," said Walter. "Now, about this 'general clutter' – just what do you suppose they're referring to?"

"It's just a guess," I said, "but they could mean those piles of scrap lumber."

"Scrap lumber?" said Walter. "Where?"

"Well," I said, "what's that?" and pointed to a heap of ragged shingles, shattered clapboards and split two-by-fours.

"That's my kindling."

"Oh. And that over there?" Boards of random length and width lay in a hopeless jumble.

"Repair parts. Table or chair breaks, got to have something to fix it with."

"And that?" I indicated another mound of broken, twisted lumber.

"That's my ice house."

"It is?"

"Yes, sir. Blew down last March. Just needs a couple days' work to set it right. Ain't that so, Luther?"

"Yes," said Luther.

"Then why don't you fix it?" I asked.

"What for? Can't cut ice in July."

"I see," I said, and I did see. "Well, maybe they mean all those plumbing fixtures over there. Take that washing machine, for example."

"Oh," said Walter, "that ain't mine."

"No?"

"No. Belongs to Ellen Gridley. Told her I'd fix it, just as soon as I get the parts."

"And the sink and bathtub?"

"Got those out of the Twombly place, after it burned down."

"Perhaps you should get rid of them, if you're not going to use them," I suggested.

"Can't. Promised them to Ed Sewall for his new house. He's already got the foundation poured. Expects to move in next spring."

"And the electric water heater?" I asked. Walter's house has never been wired for electricity, and he swears it never will be, at least as long as he's in it.

"Got that off Bill Seekins last fall, when his well dried up.

Going to swap it with Perley White for a couple of hogs he's fattening."

"Well," I said, "that pretty much accounts for everything. Except, perhaps, that pile of garbage over there." I pointed to a mound of coffee grounds and orange peels that lay mouldering beside the rusty Ford.

"That," said Walter with dignity, "is my compost heap."

***Cheryl Haynes** has written a whole collection of stories featuring Walter. Her last known address was in Searsport.*

Eleanor Henderson

SERVICE

A local storekeeper, well known for his lack of patience, sold gasoline on the side. Usually his customers bought their gas, paid up, and left. On this particular morning, he was summoned to the gas pump by a series of loud toots. Taking his time, he slowly walked out to wait on them. All talking at once, they stated they were in a hurry and for him to get a move on, they didn't have all day.

"What do you want?"

"Gas."

"Gas? By the racket you're making it don't seem that you need any gas. You're gassed up already." He pumped the gas, then upon their demand wiped the windshield and checked the oil and the battery, and wiped off the headlights. By that time he had had it.

Accepting the pay for the gas, he leaned toward the driver and said, "Don't you want me to kiss you goodbye?"

***Eleanor Henderson** died in 1980 at her home in Skowhegan.*

Alice True Larkin

HOW'D YE' KNOW I CAME FROM MAINE?

You really have to move out of the state of Maine and then move back again to fully appreciate that Maine people talk differently. Not funny, just differently. I first encountered this fact at the age of nineteen when I went down to Boston, armed only with forty dollars, the prospects of a job, and the hearty Maine adage that "As long as you've got a tongue in your head, and know how to use it, you'll make out."

I managed to stay lost for 37 days despite this sapient philosophy, and most of the forty dollars went for cab fares to extricate me from some cobblestoned labyrinth and deposit me back at my lodgings. But that is another story. I also discovered that every time that I did use the tongue in my head, no matter how facilely, someone either fell over in a fit of hysteria, or stared back at me blankly.

People exploded into embarrassing guffaws when I said "Bang-gaw," but I couldn't get my tongue around that final "r", so most of the time I avoided the word. I had only referred to Bangor as a point of reference for Skowhegan, my home town. Not many people have ever heard of Skowhegan. The secretary in one office where I was making out an application actually came out from behind the desk and did a little soft-shoe routine to a song about an old farmer "way up in Skowhegan, Maine." She said her uncle had taught her the song and dance but she hadn't ever thought there really was a place called Skowhegan.

I filled out a lot of applications in the years I lived in Boston, and I got used to writing down Skowhegan as my birthplace. Even the ribbing I took wasn't so bad after I realized that I had just missed, by about five blessed miles, being born in a town called Cornville. If I had had to write Cornville, Maine, on an application in order to get a job, I think I would have chosen prostitution.

For a long time after I got married and moved to Connecticut, our neighbors thought I called my husband "Paw." They knew his name was Paul, but they also knew I was from Maine and thought it was a quaint Downeast custom. When they said "Paul," they worked their mouth all around like a fellow with a blackberry seed under his lower plates, and after awhile I got so I could do that. I began being more careful about pronouncing my "r's", and eventually nobody thought much about my being from Maine.

When we moved back to Maine, nine years later, my mother said she couldn't understand a word the children said. They had a lot to learn, too. One of the girls appealed to me when her grandmother asked her to sweep off the piazza. She didn't mind sweeping it, but she didn't know what it was. She didn't know what a "spider" was, either. Next day, June, the oldest girl, came rushing in, all excited, with something in a paper bag. "Rolled oats," she said proudly. "I said I'd never had any, so Jenny's mother gave me some to take home." When we spilled the contents into a dish, June was crestfallen. "Why," she said, "it isn't anything but oatmeal."

At a church supper, the talk turned to fiddlehead greens and an out-of-state visitor was enthralled when the woman sitting next to him cautioned that you had to be careful not to cook

them too long or they would be salvy. His delight at this mental picture was equalled by mine when I first heard the explanation that someone hadn't been over because they had been "right out straight." This is a common expression, but I still get a fleeting vision of a woman scurrying into a sou'west gale, her skirts and apron whipping out behind her.

Also delightfully graphic is the euphemism for a distressing ailment known locally as the "back-door trots." This expression is usually delivered with a sly sideways look in front of strangers because it is considered to be somewhat of an inside joke. Outsiders think Maine people don't have outdoor privies anymore, but an awful lot of them do. They just don't brag about them. Nowadays outhouses, or "backhouses" as they are more commonly called, are generally considered to be a temporary arrangement, but their characteristics remain the same: the sensation from below on a blustery winter night, and the cantankerous nature of the things to develop a leak in the roof where the drops land right on the back of your neck. Unless, of course, you are leaning forward.

The first night that the temperature plunged to below zero after our return to Maine, I encountered the idiom that fascinates me the most. One of the water pipes – and the hot water pipe at that – ran close to an outside wall and during the night it froze. It took most of the morning to thaw it out. About noontime, the milkman stomped in, blowing on his hands, and observed my husband raring around with a blowtorch in one hand and a wet rag in the other. The wet rag is to avoid burning the house down while running a blowtorch flame along 20 feet of frozen pipes in the walls.

"Well," the milkman remarked casually, "I see your pipes 'caught' last night." I opened my mouth to retort that to my mind they were frozen tighter'n hell, but I shut it again. I had forgotten the Maine penchant for understatement.

Unfortunately, some of Maine's richest language is in danger of being lost. It has been some time since anyone has told me they "clum up a ladder," picked "rozenberries," or had sore "gooms," and the old fellow I knew who used to "go to town to do his tradin' " is long gone.

I'm as guilty as anyone of letting some of these treasures go by the board. I hardly ever threaten to send my kids "downriver" (to Thomaston State Prison) if they misbehave, and I even neglect that priceless expression of undetermined origin that describes someone who is big, clumsy, and oafish as being "gorm-ing."

Nevertheless, when I moved back to Maine I dropped my acquired Boston-Connecticut accent like a hot rock and slid happily back into my native tongue. When I procrastinate, I assure myself that I will do the job "when the spirit moves me," and if someone does it for me meanwhile, I'm "much obliged." I announce that I am going "upstreet" with impunity, and when I get back home, I wash my "hay-uh" and rinse it with "vinaguh and wa-tuh." So far I have two bushel baskets of dropped "r's" in the woodshed and I only coax them back into my vocabulary when I go out of state or brush up on my Spanish, where a final "r" does make a difference. I still remember the shuddering frustration of the teacher who taught Spanish in Skowhegan High School. "Lip lazy," she called us, but I've come to believe that Maine people are just more relaxed. Did you ever notice how jumpy New Yorkers are, and the way they chew up their words?

Coming back to Maine and Maine talk was as satisfying as slipping my Dad's old blue-denim jumper over my shoulders and walking out under the stars to the barn to listen to the gentle shifting, munching, and murmur of the cattle in the tie-up. I knew I was back home when a half-forgotten friend hailed me.

"By the gorries!" he said. "I haven't seen you since the Marimichi fire! How've ye' been?"

Alice True Larkin *lives in Boothbay Harbor with her husband and six children. She is the author of* Charlie the Crow, *and is presently working on two novels as well as being employed part time in the records department of St. Andrew's Hospital in Boothbay Harbor.*

Elizabeth Nieuwland

ON DOORS

A common disorder of cats is the Front-Door, Back-Door Complex. This is a belief, pathetically clung to through the generations, that THE WEATHER AT THE BACK DOOR IS DIFFERENT THAN THE WEATHER AT THE FRONT DOOR.

If out front the temperature is 20 below, an 80 mile an hour wind is blowing, and the snow is 10 feet high, then the cats are convinced the back door, when opened, will reveal a semi-tropical day, with a balmy 75 degree temperature. Also throw in the palm trees gently swaying in the breeze.

A well-trained owner will considerately run from one door to the other until the cats are convinced of the severity of the weather at both doors and perhaps condescend to the potty box in the basement.

Anyone who lives with cats is faced with the problem of doors. Vacations and weekends are no problem, the human can station himself at one door and post a friend or relative at the back door. I have three cats which necessitates a lot of opening and closing of doors.

However, how does one cope when the workweek comes

along? Either the cats stay out all day or in all day. This is not a satisfactory situation. Get a patented door? What if one cat decided to come in at the same time the other cat decided to leave? Could they get stuck?

I think I have solved this problem. I have hired a senior citizen, a former doorman at the Waldorf-Astoria. He sits at the front door all day and assists the cats in and out. The small sum I pay him supplements his pitiful pension and he feels useful and needed. I had a bit of difficulty at first; he insisted on hailing taxis, but we worked out a compromise. I allow him to wear his uniform and he has promised to stop flagging down cabs.

Elizabeth Nieuwland *is divorced and lives in Old Orchard Beach. A graduate of the University of Maine, she is the author of* Equal Time, *and is a columnist for the* Biddeford Journal. *She has one married daughter.*

Mavis Patterson

JAKE OUTWITS THE SHRINK

Jake might have been a sad character in many ways but there was no question that he was clever and quick-witted. One night he and some of his drinking buddies were sitting on the front porch of his grandmother's general store and one of the guys asked him to tell them what it had been like to be an inmate at South Windham.

"Well," Jake started slowly, grinning to himself, "It's a little like being a guinea pig in one of those laboratories. They got guards that keep a chart on everything you do. If you're on good behavior you get dessert at night; if you're bad you get hosed down in the morning. Then they got shrinks that are trying to learn about human behavior by asking all kinds of crazy questions.

"The second time I was at South Windham they thought I ought to have something called a Psychiatric Evaluation to decide what was making me act out so. I was taken to this room that was bare except for a grey metal table, you know, the kind with the green vinyl top, and two grey metal chairs. I musta' sat for half an hour or better and was just thinking that it was time to leave when a short, round man with a black moustache and silver rimmed glasses entered.

"'I'm Doctor Rothstein,' he said.

"'I'm Jake Cookson,' I said, holding out my hand. He didn't shake. The doctor sat opposite me at the table.

"'O.K., Jake. Today we're going to play a fantasy game.'

"'Great, Doc. I love games.'

"'Now, let's pretend that you're out in a sailboat, enjoying the sunset before heading back to shore.'

"'I'm scared of the water, Doc.'

"'It's a game, Jake, remember?'

"'O.K. Doc, you're the boss.'

"'Suddenly you find yourself surrounded by battleships. What would you do?'

"'I'd torpedo the bastards!'

"'Where would you get the torpedoes, Jake?'

"'The same place you got the battleships, Doc.'"

POPULAR STOVEPIPE

Newall Beam tells about the Pense family who lived down the road from his family on the Cove Road in Cutler. Harold and Lizanne, and their children Harold Jr. and Hense were extremely poor and uneducated. Harold stuttered, especially when he was nervous or excited or riled up in general. The Penses were the subject of many a local joke. They lived in a little house that didn't have a chimney, so Harold just stuck a stove pipe out a window. Passers by would ask, "Say, Harold, does your stove draw good?"

Harold replied seriously, "O-o-oh, yes, it d-d-draws the attention of every damned fool who goes by here."

MORE PENSE

Hense and Harold Jr. would do almost anything for a little spending money. They cleaned yards, picked up wood, and were always available for odd jobs around town. One day, with some money in their pockets, they showed up in Charlie Smith's store. Hense wanted a hammer and Harold wanted one, too.

Charlie, knowing how poor the family was, suggested, "Now look, Harold, Hense is buying a hammer and I'll bet he'd let you use it when you wanted. Instead of you buying one too, why don't you buy a can of beans or something to put on the table?"

Harold, having inherited a stutter from his father said, "Say, Ch-Ch-Charlie, did you ever try to d-drive a nail with a can of beans?"

YOU KNOW THOSE SECOND HAND CARS

Newall's favorite joke was one he heard from one of the cookies in the lumber camp. The cookie had grown up in Southern Georgia and moved north when his mother, who was a Maine native, inherited her parents' farm down Machias way. He told about a man who worked for a wealthy Southerner and had saved enough money to buy himself a second hand car. His boss came up to him one morning, impressed with the new purchase.

"Hear you bought yourself a new car, Sam?"

"Yes suh, yes, suh."

"Does she run good, Sam?"

"No suh, can't say it do."

"What seems to be the problem, Sam?"

"Well, Boss, you know the motor?"

"Yes."

"Well, it don't mote so good."

"Why not?"

"Well, Boss, you know the carbulator?"

"Yes, I know the carburetor."

"Well, it don't carb. And the genulator?"

"Yes, the generator."

"It don't gen. And you know the pistons?"

"Yes."

"Well, they don't work so good either."

A MOTHER'S CONCERN

Some of Gordon Costley's family settled south of Lewiston, somewhere around the Royal River. His mother used to tell of an old woman who was such a tarter that she drove her husband off, and all the children, with the exception of one, left as soon as they were old enough to find work.

One day Liza realized that she had run out of tea and sent Jamie out in a howling blizzard to get some from the local store which was a couple of miles away. Although Jamie protested he figured it was less painful to follow Liza's orders than to listen to her rant and rave all night.

On his return, Jamie decided to take a short cut across the river and fell through a fishing hole. After a brief search his body was found, brought home, and laid out in the parlor. Liza cried and cried and when she was at last able to get hold of herself she grabbed her boy's hand, tears streaming down her wrinkled cheeks and said, "Jamie, Jamie, my son. Just one word, that's all I ask of yuh. Where'd yuh drop my tea?"

GOVERNING THE HEAT

Ira Taylor, of Sidney, used to tell of a fella who was always bragging about his cookstove, how good it was and what a great draft it had. In addition to this fine piece, he also possessed the profanest tongue on the River Road.

"One time I put some wood in 'er, opened the draft as wide as it would go, and by Jeezus it drew itself right up to the ceiling and hung there kicking itself around for three days until it cooled off enough to settle back down on the hearth where it belonged."

A neighbor who was the recipient of this description told him, "Why, you'll have to put a governor on that thing before it takes you up in smoke."

"Governor, hell!" the proud owner yelled. " 'Twould need the President of the United States himself to keep that thing down."

WHAT'S A DEAD COW WORTH, ANYWAY?

Dr. Beckerman stood New York City just about as long as he could, then moved to Maine with his new wife, bought a large farm in Sidney, where his wife had spent all of her childhood, and set up his practice in the neighboring city of Waterville. He kept a few cows on the side and used to boast to his colleagues about how much milk he was getting. This amused his wife immensely. Having grown up on a farm, this was old hack to her, but to the doc, every new piece of equipment was a toy calling for a celebration, and every new cow was like a new baby.

The cows were pastured across the road from the farm and one evening as they were crossing to the barn at milking time, a big El Dorado with New York plates came speeding through, neglectful of the crossing cows. There was a screeching of tires, and the car hit one of Doc's prized Jerseys broadside. There she lay, bleeding all over the tar, dead as a doornail.

The driver, a woman dressed in a three-piece pin-striped suit, jumped out, excited and trembling.

"Did I harm it? Did I harm it? If I did I'll gladly pay for damages!"

Doc, more flustered than the city slicker, replied boisterously, "Well if you did 'er any damned good, I'll pay *you* for it!"

HOW TO EXTRACT MILK

Lodgie LeClair was caretaker for the Skowhegan School of Art and Sculpture for thirty years or more. In addition to caring for the grounds he pastured a few milk cows.

Students came to summer classes from all over the world and Lodgie took great pleasure in telling them tall tales. One summer two girls from Chicago were in residence; neither had ever seen a cow. One of them walked up to Lodgie one day and asked, "How do you extract milk, Mr. LeClair?"

"How do you *what,* Sarah?"

"How do you extract milk?"

"Well, first of all, it's called *milking* a cow, and if you'd like a first-hand demonstration, you come back at four-thirty this afternoon and you can see for yourself."

Sarah ran off, excited, calling to her city friend, "Jane! Jane! Mr. LeClair is going to show me how to extract milk this afternoon. Do you want to watch?"

That afternoon Lodgie found his assistant, Joe, and asked him to find Jessie, the oldest and most patient of the milkers.

"I want you to tie her to that apple tree out behind the tool shed. We're going to show those Chicago girls how to milk."

The girls came along just as Joe was tying Jessie up and as they stood watching, their eyes lit up. They were twittering as excitedly as any young girl on her first date.

"O.K., Joe," Lodgie said, picking up Jessie's tail, "I'm gonna prime 'er. When I've pumped 'er fifteen times you get ready to milk." Joe was an old milker from way back and sat like an expert on the milking stool waiting for the prime to take.

Lodgie pumped Jessie's tail fifteen times and Joe started milking. The girls watched, fascinated.

"Oh, Mr. LeClair, can we try it? Can we try it?"

"Of course you can. Ain't nothing to it. Sit yourself right down here. I'll prime and you milk." Lodgie pumped again and the girl pinched the teats, one at a time, but no milk came. Disappointed, she asked, "What am I doing wrong?"

"Oh, it just takes a little practice," Lodgie assured her. "Joe and I have been milking since we was younger than you. It just kinda' comes to you natural after a while."

The girls walked off and Lodgie and Joe had a good laugh. A couple of days later, Mrs. Cummings, owner of the school, came upon the girls. They had old Jessie tied to the apple tree; one of them was pumping like hell and the other was pinching. Still no milk.

"What on earth are you doing?" shrieked Mrs. Cummings.

"We're trying to extract milk just like Mr. LeClair showed us. But we aren't having any luck."

"Oh," said Mrs. Cummings, familiar with Lodgie's pranks, "That's because you don't have the bucket under her."

TROUT FISHING

Lodgie LeClair and a friend of his, Ed McLaughlin, spent a long Labor Day weekend on a fishing trip some years ago on Lake Parlin on Route 201 on the way to Quebec City. They rented one of the small camps and got up early the first day to fish. They loaded up their gear, worms, a basket of lunch and plenty of cold beer and set out for a day of serious fishing. They stayed on the water all day and at dusk came back empty handed. The second day they got up early again and headed out; and at dusk returned long-faced. They had caught one small trout.

Little Joe, the owner of the camps, was a man in his late seventies. The second evening the boys were there he wandered over to their campsite and asked how the fish were biting.

"Not so good," Ed said. "Two full days of fishing and only one scrawny trout to show for it. We were just thinking that we'd pack up and head back to Skowhegan tomorrow."

"Tell you what," Little Joe said, "I'll get a buddy of mine to watch the camps tomorrow and I'll take you boys to a place where you can get all the trout you want, and then some." The boys were skeptical but agreed to meet him at the main camp next morning at 5:30.

Little Joe was waiting for them. The guys were loaded down with their usuals but all Little Joe carried was a baseball bat. Ed and Lodgie looked at each other but neither said a word. Surely he would pick up at least a pole somewhere along the way.

Little Joe led and the boys followed, through the woods, over a stream up a hill, and down the other side. At the bottom lay a small pond, calm and clear. A boat was beached and tied to a tree; the boys put it into the water and all climbed in. Little Joe rowed them out to the center of the pond and pulled in the oars. The boys assembled their gear, baited their hooks, and settled down to fish, not very enthusiastically. Little Joe sat back, reached into his shirt pocket and pulled out a plug of B&L chewing tobacco. By this time the boys were convinced that he wasn't going to fish, that he was just going to row them around. Little Joe pulled out a jackknife, cut off a piece of tobacco and rubbed it in the palms of his hands until it was in small bits. Then he spread it out over the water on either side of the boat and sat back in his seat with his arms crossed over his chest.

Pretty soon the water began to boil and the trout began to jump. One after the other they grabbed the tobacco and dove back to the bottom of the pond to chew. Ed and Lodgie couldn't believe their eyes, but the water was so clear that they could look down and see the fish chewing nonchalantly. Well, when you chew, sooner or later you have to spit, and after a few minutes the fish began to surface. Up they jumped, and

there was Little Joe, ready with the bat. The instant the first one pursed its lips he hit it over the head. The boys grabbed it and threw it into the bottom of the boat. The other fish followed suit, and it all happened so fast that within five minutes the bottom of the boat was covered with so many trout that the boat slowly sank to the bottom and off swam their catch.

HOW TO CATCH A DRUNK

Soloman Thatcher was known around Falmouth as the town drunk. Late one evening, on his return from his favorite saloon, Solomon fell through the ice of the farmer's pond that bordered his place. The farmer heard Solomon yell twice, ran out to where the cry came from, and arrived at the pond just in time to see Solomon's red stocking cap disappear under the ice. He called the sheriff who arrived with a dozen men. All agreed that there wasn't much that could be done, that there was no great loss, and they might just as well wait until Spring to drag the bottom. The farmer, however, felt differently. "Solomon's a harmless sort. I think we owe it to our conscience to at least find the body."

At that, one of the other men spoke up, "I know how to find him. You got any whiskey at your place?" he asked the farmer.

"I do."

"Why don't you fetch it, and bring a rope along?" The farmer looked puzzled but went back to the house and returned with the requested items. The man took the cap off the whiskey bottle, tied the rope around its neck and lowered it into the hole where Solomon had disappeared. All stood around, some chuckling under their breath, some with a question on their faces. In less than a flash they saw a mittened hand grab the line and up they pulled. At the end was old Solomon with the jug in his mouth, hanging on for dear life.

PIG MAN

Albert Greenleaf was a good father, a good provider, and according to his pudgy wife, Ethel, a not so good husband; but his first love was his pigs. Albert was considered the authority in Sidney as far as pigs went. People even came from neighboring towns to ask his advice, especially in matters of breeding. Albert was a man of few words and some said he didn't have any social conscience. He was seldom seen out and about except for an occasional trip to Hodgson's General Store and regular attendance at the annual town meeting.

As is the case in many small towns, nicknames are secretly given to any person whose private life has any mystery about it. Albert was known around town as Pig Man. The kids at the Elementary School had even made up a rope skipping jingle about him.

Pig Man, oh Pig Man
Where are you going?
To the auction to buy some more shoats?
Pig Man, oh Pig Man
Your sows are so smelly
Wouldn't you rather raise goats?

Although Albert never let on, he knew that he was the topic of many a clandestine conversation and was rather amused to think that he could provide some sort of entertainment to the townspeople without even trying.

Albert's care of his pigs was almost ceremonial. Each night he collected swill from Glad Acres Rest Home on the Pond Road and at the school and boiled it to make sure that it didn't get rancid. He claimed that nothing presented more of a health hazard to pigs than rancid swill. The buckets were sterilized after each feeding and covered with tissue paper, a tip he had picked up at a fancy hotel that covered its toilet seats, the time he attended a two day conference on Alternative Diets for Pigs in up-state New York. Albert didn't have any hobbies to speak of, but Ethel swore he had leanings toward gourmet cooking as was evidenced by the endless variety of creative concoctions that he made up for his pigs. His favorite recipe called for 12 quarts of Elementary swill, 8 quarts of Glad Acres, and a dozen cracked eggs from John Ernst's chicken farm. To this he added just enough tepid water to make it slosh around in the bucket. Every night after supper he polished the swill buckets with such care that you would have thought that he had apprenticed as a Tiffany clerk.

Albert never called Sue-e-e like other pig farmers but instead trilled Lee-la, Lee-la as he walked to the sty. Sure enough, when he got to the sty the pigs were always lined up waiting for chow. Sometimes on a warm summer evening, Albert would walk back to the sty and play the pigs a tune on his tin whistle. He claimed that the music aided in the digestive process and calmed the pigs down so that they got a good night's sleep. This was particularly important after the sows had farrered as they sometimes got restless in the night and rolled over squashing the babies under their heavy carcasses. Each pig had a name, carefully chosen, and Albert talked lovingly about them all as if they were his own offspring. The old folks at the rest home were so familiar with their names that they would often ask, "How's Molly's cystitis?" or "How's Abby's appetite nowadays?"

As Spring rolled around each year, Albert submitted an ad to his favorite magazine, *Uncle Henry's Swap and Shop,* published in Rockland, which read:

> Looking for quality boar to breed two high-quality sows. Must be of excellent caliber, have a pleasing personality and come with at least two references. Will offer pick of litter in exchange of services. No sloppy pigs need apply.

When Albert Greenleaf died, the Maine Pig Growers Association had published in the Waterville Morning Sentinel a memorial which read:

> In loving memory of Albert Greenleaf – a good friend, a gentleman, and a fine judge of pigs.

Mavis Patterson *lives in Sidney with her son, Fred, in a house she designed and built herself. She is a medical social worker in Augusta and a published poet.*

Debbie Richards

THE GREAT PIG CHASE

The day was cold and rainy – typical October weather. I was just recovering from sacking home a week's worth of groceries for four kids, whose main purpose in life was to eat us out of house and home, when I discovered that my two little pigs had gotten out. Let it here be explained that a two-month-old pig is a white tornado on cloven hooves. They are faster than a Triple Crown winner, more obstinate than a Missouri mule, and when (and if) caught, more noisy than a six-year-old blender on "puree."

When I went out to try to corner my little terrors, it was discovered, to my hysteria, that my big pig, fondly called Freezer Bound, was out, too.

Let me be merciful to myself and just say that in the process of trying to retrieve my swine, I got soaked in the rain, lost a boot in the mud, fell flat in a pile of pig muck, and got nipped (more than once) by the electric fence.

Enter on the scene Mr. M., the custodian at the school. He was bringing home our prodigal pup who was always running off. Mr. M., after hitching the dog back up, eagerly entered the Great Pig Chase.

By employing a great deal of teamwork, strategy, and placing pig grain in tempting spots, we managed to return all of the pigs to their proper abodes. What remains most vividly in my mind is Mr. M's laconic comment, repeated often during our maneuvers, "Ayuh, by God, you can work with a cow or a hoss, but you can't do a friggin' thing with a hawg."

Debbie Richards *of New Sharon is married and has four children. She works in the woods, twitching logs and stacking pulp, and is a member of the Volunteer Fire Department.*

Dyan Sawtelle

FARMING IN THE OLD DAYS

The first Sawtelle reunion I attended was when I was twenty-six years old. Although acquainted with most of Father's family, I had never spent any time with them because they lived out of state and as a child "out of state" meant you never went to visit. We rarely saw any of them except when they came to Maine for short visits.

The first thing that I noticed was the resemblance of body structure and facial expressions of the Sawtelle men. All had large noses (Father once said that as a child I told him that I would like to have all the nickels he could hold in his nose), were tall and slightly paunched, and when standing, folded their arms and rocked back and forth on their feet.

The second thing that I noticed as a striking resemblance was their sense of humor, both men and women. Each competed with the others, faces expressionless, to tell the tallest tale. Each story had a strain of the "old days" running through it.

We had just sat down to eat. There were twenty-seven of us and we surrounded the three long cafeteria tables borrowed from the West River Road Firehouse in Sidney where my parents lived and where my two sisters and I had returned to live after a few years away. Cousin David started in when I passed him a plate of tomatoes.

"You grow these?"

"No, Father did."

"Jeezus, ain't they scrawny looking things?" he nudged his sister, Dot.

"What d'ya mean, scrawny?" Father said defensively. "These are the biggest tomatoes in town. Planted 'em in the old pig pen."

"Hm," David grunted, looking at his other sister, Caddie. "Cad, you remember the tomatoes we used to plant on the farm? They were so huge that you needed a tripod, a chain fall, and a good-sized wheelbarrow to carry one home in."

"Yup, that's right," Caddie confirmed. "Then we had to use a cross cut saw to slice it. One tomato fed a family of eight for a week."

Mother passed a plate of cucumbers to Caddy. "You grow these, too, Vera?" Caddie asked.

"Yes."

"Boy these look good. Speaking of cukes, these remind me

of the summer we planted cucumbers that grew faster and wilder than the rest of the garden. Why, the vines grew so fast that we had to put roller skates on the cukes so's the vines wouldn't drag 'em to death."

Dyan Sawtelle *of Oakland is single and actively involved in women's rights issues. She works as a carpenter and writes poetry.*

Vera Sawtelle

A LOGICAL PLACE FOR A FIRE

As a child I lived in the small town of Fairfield Center where little excitement was to be found. Crime was low and it was safe to be out on the street at night. Often I could be found with my friends under the street light in front of Albert Holt's store playing hopscotch. During the day we occasionally snuck under the cider mill in the center of town where we would smoke cigarettes that Reg Campbell, the most daring of the group, had obtained in some mysterious way not known to the rest of us.

Reg could be dared into almost anything but usually didn't need any encouragement.

One afternoon as we sat puffing under the mill, Reg excused himself. "I have a small matter to tend to. I'll be back in a few minutes. Don't smoke all the cigarettes, you hear?"

A half hour passed and Reg appeared. But instead of joining us he walked across the street to Albert's and stood as if waiting for someone. Shortly there arrived a fire truck, its bell clanging and the men prepared to find fire. The truck stopped and the chief yelled to Reg, "Where's the fire, young man?"

Reg grinned, tipped his cap back, took his time and answered, "Why, in the cookstove, I suppose."

GIVE THE POOR PRINCE A BREATHER, WILL YA?

Timothy Brown was the owner of a small store in Fairfield Center where I grew up. Tim was a moody fellow and didn't take too fondly to kids, making him the subject of many a prank.

Bob MacKay and his brother, Skinny, disliked Tim immensely. They were always and forever coming up with suggestions to antagonize the old man. One afternoon, when Mama and Papa were off to Fairfield to do errands, Bob and Skinny stopped by to use the phone.

"Who you calling?" I asked.

"Just you watch," Skinny replied with a menacing twinkle in his eye.

I watched as he dialed.

"That's Tim Brown's number!" I shrieked.

"Hush," Bob's hand went over my mouth.

"Say, Tim," Skinny began. "You got Prince Albert in the can?"

A pause.

"Well, for Christ's sake, let him out for air, will ya?"

Vera Sawtelle *lives in Sidney with her husband. The mother of three daughters, she does private duty nursing at area hospitals and keeps a journal.*

Arlene Smart

THE PHANTOM LADY OF PLANTATION #21

Tucked away in a remote corner of Washington County, Maine, dwelled a postage stamp community called Plantation #21. Though Time and Progress had left their marks, few changes were ever seen. Formal schooling was a passing fancy, but life was rounded out by personal dignity, patriotism, and a good dose of the sense of ridiculous, the latter being an aid in the day to day struggle for survival.

Town Meeting was a once-a-year shebang and everyone attended from miles around. It was said that no better form of entertainment was known in that neck of the woods. Among the interested citizens was a fellow by the name of Jeanie Hump. Now Jeanie stood a good six axe handles tall and was pole bean skinny. He had to stand twice to cast a shadow, as they say. Jeanie had two wives: Lottie, and her sister Abigail. They sold butter and eggs. Between them they tipped the freight scale at 410 pounds, and this was without their aprons and caps. Jeanie sat between them at the Town Meeting, a whisker of a thing peeking out from beneath folds of flesh and skirt.

"Mr. Moderator," says Jeanie, standing tall. "I see here time and time again in the Annual Report money paid out to some woman called Mis-cellaneous. I don't seem to know her, and I've lived in Plantation Number 21 for fifty-three years; I'd like to make a motion that we pay her off once and for all and get her the hell off the books!"

Needless to say, this broke up the meeting and the people in Plantation #21 still chuckle about the mysterious woman who would still be bleeding the town dry if it hadn't been for Jeanie Hump.

Arlene Smart *is single and lives in Skowhegan. She is a painter, and is not currently writing.*

Lucy Thomas

GALLIVANTING BEES

My husband's Uncle Fred was a Winslow boy and grew up across from the Smileys who had a large herd of milk cows and operated a dairy business. Uncle Fred also farmed but on a smaller scale as he was more interested in the politics of the town. At one time he was Third Selectman and another time the Road Commissioner. When he rode around the farm and the back roads he drove his old white Ford, but when he went into town he drove his shiny black and chrome Chrysler, which was sleek and smooth as an unrippled pond.

Uncle Fred's hobby was keeping bees and he was as proud of those bees as some folks are of their children. Whenever anyone came to visit he first gave them a tour of his hives, which numbered at least twenty, then a tour of the many jars of honey which he kept in the summer kitchen.

One person who wasn't a bit impressed with Uncle Fred's hobby was Mr. Smiley. One day he called Fred over and asked, "Would you mind keeping your bees at home? They're bothering my cows something awful."

"You sure they're my bees?" Fred asked.

"You're the only one raises bees around here that I know of,"

Mr. Smiley replied, a bit irritated.

"Well," Fred chuckled, "if you're so convinced that they're really mine, why don't you just send them home?"

WHAT'S IN A REMEDY?

Wilton Black and his family had been farming in Winthrop a good many years and were always consulted when any of the neighboring folk had a problem with their critters or gardens. In the early 60's a lot of young people moved into the area from Boston and New York City and set up farming. Most of them had never raised a garden and a couple had never seen a cow before. The established residents jokingly referred to them as "textbook farmers."

One day one of the new young men drove over to Wilton's place in his beat up Volkswagen and asked what to do for potato bugs.

"Well," drawled Wilton, "I only had 'em once and I used wood ashes."

"Did you sprinkle them *on* the plants or *around* the plants?"

"I sprinkled them on the plants."

"Thanks," said the young man and drove off.

A week later the man returned. "What was it you said you put on your potato plants when they had bugs?" he asked.

"Wood ashes," Wilton answered.

"Hmm," the fellow said, "that's strange. That's just what I did, and they killed my potatoes."

"Ayuh," Wilton chuckled, "they killed mine, too."

A FINE SET OF GRINDERS

During the 50s, in winter months, Roy Hutchins and his friends got together every Saturday night to play cards and swap stories. They took turns meeting at each other's houses. The wives attended but always met separately from the men to drink tea and share handcrafts.

One night Roy came to the table sporting a new set of teeth. Comments and praises passed around and finally Ed Daggett, who had grown up with Roy in Lubec said, "Say Roy, do you remember Bud Young?"

"Sure do."

"You know," Ed said to the rest of the men, "Roy's new teeth remind me of a funny story about Bud. Roy and I used to hang around the country store with the boys when we were youngsters, whittling, telling yarns, sneaking a chew of tobacco, and all. One day Bud came walking down the road, all dressed up.

" 'Where you off to?' I asked him.

" 'To Calais to get myself some new choppers.'

" 'You walking all the way?'

" 'Nope, gonna take the train.'

"A few more words were exchanged and Bud headed off to the depot.

"Late that same afternoon, the train pulled in and we boys were all eagerly standing around waiting to see Bud in his new choppers.

" 'Well, did you get 'em?' Albert Taylor asked.

" 'Ayuh.'

" 'Where are they?' Albert pried, the rest of us anxious but not so brazen.

" 'Right here in this box,' Bud replied.

" 'In the box?' Albert pressed. 'How come you don't have them in?' "

" 'Have them in?' Bud looked puzzled. 'Have them in where?' "

" 'Why, in your mouth, of course. That's where most people put their choppers, ain't it? Don't do no good tucked away in a box. Besides you have to wear them and get used to them.'

"With that Bud began to chuckle and opened the box that was tied up neatly with a piece of twine and pulled out a food grinder.

" 'That ain't no set of false teeth,' I said.

" 'Who said anything about false teeth?' Bud asked. 'I said I was going to Calais to get a new chopper.' "

***Lucy Thomas** is married and lives in Benton, where she is active in the Grange, church, and Daughters of the American Revolution.*

Diana C. Young

LOYALTY IN MAINE

I wasn't enthusiastic about learning to drive in the first place, and I promised myself a few years back, when circumstances forced me to get my license, that at least I would never drive in Boston. No way. Why is it, then, that any such rigid stance becomes an irresistible challenge to fate? Within months, my family commitments had made hash of my resolve.

I, a Connecticut native, am married to Cracker Jack Jones, citizen of the Pine Tree State and to his family of one mother, two brothers, three sisters-in-law, two "ex," four sisters, five brothers-in-law, one deceased, eight nieces and nine nephews.

One of our sisters, Earleen Jones, lived in Boston, in an overpriced basement hovel, and one day she decided she had had enough. After ten years acquaintance with the place, she wanted to go back home in the worst way. She left her hovel for good and moved to the family seat in Happy Hollow, Maine.

She moved all of her furniture, utensils and knick knacks in a U-Haul with the help of some Wampanaug Indians, a vaguely inaccurate but certainly colorful crew. In the rush to be off, she neglected her ancient station wagon, Cockroach, who had calfed in an alley at the rear of her place in the Finkbein Apartments. Mrs. Finkbein informed Earleen that if the car still reposed there by August first, it would be hauled away.

At first, Earleen was happy enough to be rid of the heap because as well as a healthy dollop of rust and other ailments too numerous to mention, it hadn't the benefit of brakes. But as the weeks wore on toward the end of July, and Earleen sat denned up in Happy Hollow, with many miles of dirt roads between her and the nearest beauty parlor, she developed a nagging desire for old Cockroach.

The Cracker Jones and Co., Inc., Movers of Old Cars, was selected in spite of serious misgivings, to wrest the hulk from the sinister minions of Massachusetts and to conduct it on its matron flight to Maine. Earleen had long since lost her nerve to do the job alone, and Jack was billed as expert at driving cars without brakes through Boston traffic – the secret being to choose the right moment. In this case, the only right moment was at four o'clock on a Sunday morning, no earlier, no later, no other day of the week.

With this key to success in mind, our Dodge Coronet Wagon left up home in Happy Valley after a hearty Saturday night bean supper. (And they call *Boston* Bean Town!) Our party included Jack and Earleen, our collective nephew, Henry Hanover Jones who wanted to go along for the ride, and me. I didn't want to go along, ride or no ride, but Cracker Jack needed moral support of a kind that he trusted neither Henry H. nor Earleen to provide. Mostly this support consisted of driving the staff car on the return trip.

Our vehicle was not stopped by the border guards of the Common Poverty of Massachusetts. Little did they know that we of the magnificent and heart rending State of Maine had come to remove one of their greatest sources of revenue, an old car, a fleabag on wheels. We drove further and further into the neverland of Megalop, dodging dangerous orange barrels and flashing arrows, the mines and trip flares of Joe Green's army. His bridge and road trolls took out quarters and forty-cent pieces with the red-eyed abandon of the highly overpopulated.

Hah! We achieved the inner redoubt. We arrived at Earleen's former abode two hours short of midnight. Figuring that Mrs. Finkbein would not call out the tow truck immediately, and being quite tired from our ride, we took an easy cat nap on a scrofulous pseudo-colonial braided rug. This was the only remaining piece of "furniture" in the place except for the bathroom fixtures.

We were awakened intermittently by the shrill arguments of inebriates in the alley, and by the whispered conversations of car strippers. C. Jack got up and investigated the latter, but, unfortunately, they had left Cockroach intact.

At 3:45 in the morning of Sunday, August first, Mrs. Finkbein was already up catching the worms and making threatening statements from her bedroom window. With this incentive to be on the road, the caravan got under weigh. I am not at my best at 3:45 a.m. The skin that holds my cells together is at its most elastic and my stomach nurtures sentimental memories of morning sickness.

Be that as it may, we moved out with me driving the staff car and Earleen beside me as a guide. Cockroach, with Cracker Jack at the wheel, and Henry H. riding a drowsy shotgun, was directly behind. The streets were empty and slick with spates of rain. At the corner of God-Knows-Where and Storrow Drive, patrons of some late club, in a car which could have been Cockroach's twin, forged through the intersection, narrowly missing the red light. The staff car narrowly missed this lunatic by judicious application of disc brakes; and then, because Cracker Jack knows how and when to steer, the Cockroach narrowly missed the staff car by application of diversionary tactics.

The cavalcade continued uneventfully to an all night concession in Lynn where gas was necessary for both vehicles. When we were full up, Cockroach wouldn't start and wouldn't start. I suggested that Earleen and the men transfer the three old TV sets from her trunk to ours in the event of a sad but necessary abandonment. Earleen hugged her thumbs and rolled her eyes and before any final solution was put into effect, a violent storm let loose and poured down donder and blitzen upon us for a full hour. During this interval Cockroach cooled and when the rain let up, she started with the first try. Earleen looked triumphant and went to sit with Cracker Jack. Now that we were safely out of Boston, they took the lead. Henry H. woke up and got in with me.

Bit by bit we gained the borders. No bullets raked our flaking carapaces. No ferocious dogs fell upon us from the exit ramps of Rt. 495, and as we crossed the high bridge at Portsmouth, New Hampshire, with Maine spreading its lumpy wilderness ahead, I felt heroic and jubilant with the sight of home. I winked my lights, dot dot dot dash, "V" for victory, at Cockroach.

Cracker Jack needed his coffee so we made a brief halt off the turnpike at mile 23, a danish pastry plaza which featured no sugarless food except Fritos. We paused again at the Skowhegan McDonald's where I grabbed an Egg McMuffin. Both times Cockroach was left trembling with engine ablast in the parking lot.

Our grit-covered convoy arrived in triumph and with horns blaring at the family seat, but no one heard us since Mother Jones had the weather report turned up loud.

In the weeks since her trip, Earleen hasn't come right out with it, but she seems to have lost all interest in the beauty parlor and has denned up with renewed determination. Cockroach sits on cinder blocks down in the clearing below the sap house. Mice make nests in her upholstery and in the three TV sets in the back. And I, after catching up on some well earned sleep, have entertained a smug sense of family loyalty.

Diana C. Young *of Bangor is married and the mother of three. Besides writing humorous fiction, she is a free-lance illustrator. She is currently working on* The After-life of Adolph Hitler *and drawing sketches of homes for local real estate agencies.*